WORRY MOVES ON

by Liz Haske

Illustrated by InSong Nam

For my beloved Wolves and Dragons, big and small...
It was an honor to learn alongside you.

May you always find the Courage to try!

-Liz Haske

To my hub, DoKyu,
and my children, John and Yool

Always, thank you!

-InSong Nam

ISBN-13: 978-0999441558

Visit www.lizhaske.com to share your own story of Worry and Courage.
We would love to hear from you!

School was Sophia's happy place.

More than anything she loved to puzzle
with numbers and explore how things worked.

Learning was practically her middle name.

Sophia was a true leader in everything she did.

She was the apple of her teacher's eye.

Her parents couldn't have been prouder.

Then Worry arrived,
darkening the space in Sophia's mind.

And suddenly, Sophia wasn't Sophia anymore.

First, her mind went blank during math.

"How could I forget how to do this?
Why doesn't it make sense?"

Then, Sophia froze up during
a science investigation.

"What if my thinking is not correct?
Am I even doing this right?"

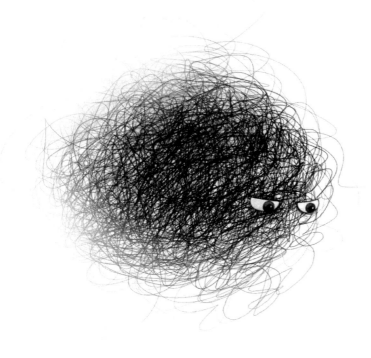

By the time the teacher asked the class to take out their writing notebooks, Sophia was so twisted up with Worry she couldn't think.

She put her head in her hands and begged the tears not to fall.

"This is too hard," she thought, "I'll never get it right."

Worry had grown so powerful that Sophia was a tangled mess.

The idea of making a mistake or not knowing how to do something filled her with so much fear she was no longer willing to try.

Sophia's teachers were puzzled.
"What's going on with Sophia?" they wondered.
"What can we do to help her?" they whispered.

And then one day, Sophia found help
in an unexpected way.

"Are you ok?" a gentle voice asked.
"You seem worried. I can help you."

Maya knew all about Worry.

She showed Sophia how
to put her hands on her belly...

and focus on her breath.

"When Worry starts to take hold, I call on Courage,"
Maya explained. "First, I notice and greet Worry.
I say, 'Hello Worry,' and use breathing to calm my mind."

Maya put her hands on her belly and grinned,
"When I breathe, sometimes I even imagine
Courage coming in and Worry going out."

Sophia listened as Maya continued, "After that, I use self-talk. That is when I act like a coach and remind myself that I am brave."

Together they practiced. Little by little, Sophia figured out how to call on Courage.

Each time Sophia tamed Worry,
Courage's power grew.

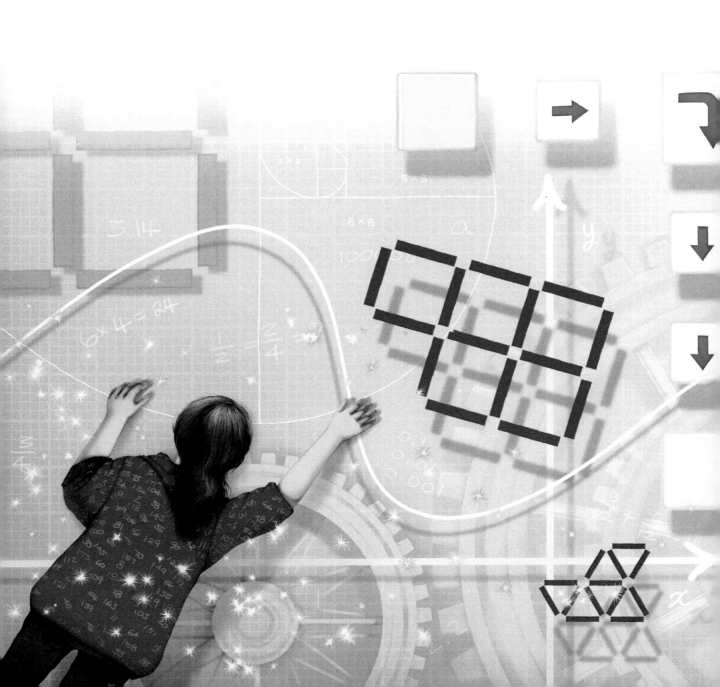

As Sophia marched into class, she noticed
that for the first time in a long time
she wasn't nervous or afraid.

Her mind didn't go blank during math.
Instead, Sophia sat up straight
and called on Courage as she said,
"I know this. I can do it if I give myself time to think."

47×18

$40 + 7$ $10 + 8$

$$
\begin{array}{r}
400 \\
320 \\
70 \\
+ \quad 56 \\
\hline
846
\end{array}
$$

$40 \quad + \quad 7$

	40		7
10	400		70
+ 8	320		56

$47 \times 18 = 846$

During science, a smile spread across her face.
"Mistakes mean that I am learning.
Even if I am not right, I will still grow."

As Sophia picked up her pencil,
Worry was ready to turn her writing project
into an impossible mountain to climb.

But then Sophia said,
"This is tricky, but I will try,"
and Worry backed off.

Reading Reflection #4

Sophia M.

For this reading reflection, I read A wrinkle in
Time by Madeleine L'En___ ___ This book
is about a twelve-year-old g___
Meg Murry, who goes off on a journey
through the galaxy with her brother,
Charles Wallace, Calvin O'Keefe, Mrs.
Whatsit, Who and Which to find her
father, who disappeared when

Sophia was beaming from head to toe.
Courage helped her feel ready to try.
Courage made it okay to make mistakes.

She didn't mind if she wasn't the expert.
Thanks to Courage, she uncovered Confidence.

With Confidence, Sophia stood taller.

She felt powerful and brave.

With her head held high,
she felt ready for anything.

Sign-Up for Science Night		
Name	**Gr.**	**Project**
John Lee	5	Electro magnet
Chloe Zhang	4	mentos
Ellie Loschan	1st	metumorfusis!
Ziyue Deu	3	Rainbow Flowers!
Daniel Heremy	5	Banana Beauty
Astoria Stimmler	5	Dancing Light

And suddenly, Worry wasn't Worry anymore.

Sophia's teachers smiled when they saw her.
"Does Sophia look more determined?" they wondered.
"What a celebration!" they whispered.

And so it was that taking risks
and making mistakes
didn't hold Sophia back
when she faced a new challenge.

Instead of wilting with Worry, she met it head on.

"Time to move on Worry...

Courage and Confidence are here."

Does Worry get in the way of your learning?

To help Worry move on you can:

Notice

"I feel worried."

Greet

"Hello, Worry."

Breathe

"Breathe Courage in...
Breathe Worry out."

Use Self-Talk

"I can do this!"

If you know how to find Courage...Pass it on!

Made in the USA
Middletown, DE
28 October 2020